DATE DUE			

The Night Before Christmas

by

Clement Clarke Moore

 illustrated by

Gennady Spirin

MARSHALL CAVENDISH
CHILDREN

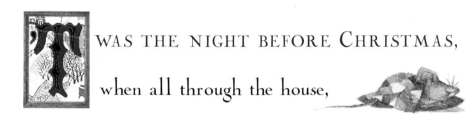

’TWAS THE NIGHT BEFORE CHRISTMAS,

when all through the house,

Not a creature was stirring, not even a mouse;

The stockings were hung by the chimney with care,

In hopes that St. Nicholas soon would be there;

The children were nestled all snug in their beds,

While visions of sugar plums danced in their heads,

And Mama in her 'kerchief, and I in my cap,

Had just settled our brains for a long winter's nap—

WHEN out on the lawn there arose such a clatter,

I sprang from the bed to see what was the matter.

Away to the window I flew like a flash,

Tore open the shutters and threw up the sash.

The moon on the breast of the new-fallen snow,

Gave the luster of midday to objects below,

When, what to my wondering eyes should appear,

But a miniature sleigh, and eight tiny reindeer.

With a little old driver, so lively and quick,

I knew in a moment it must be St. Nick.

MORE rapid than eagles his coursers they came,

And he whistled, and shouted, and called them by name.

"Now, Dasher! Now, Dancer! Now, Prancer and Vixen!

On, Comet! On, Cupid! On, Dunder and Blixem!

To the top of the porch! To the top of the wall!

Now dash away, dash away, dash away all!"

As dry leaves before the wild hurricane fly,

When they meet with an obstacle, mount to the sky,

So up to the house-top the coursers they flew,

With the sleigh full of toys–and St. Nicholas too.

13

 AND then in a twinkling, I heard on the roof

The prancing and pawing of each little hoof.

AS I drew in my head, and was turning around,

Down the chimney St. Nicholas came with a bound.

 HE was dressed all in fur, from his head to his foot,

And his clothes were all tarnished with ashes and soot;

A bundle of toys was flung on his back,

And he looked like a peddler just opening his pack.

HIS eyes–how they twinkled! His dimples, how merry.

His cheeks were like roses, his nose like a cherry.

His droll little mouth was drawn up like a bow,

And the beard of his chin was as white as the snow.

The stump of a pipe he held tight in his teeth,

And the smoke it encircled his head like a wreath.

He had a broad face, and a little round belly

That shook when he laughed, like a bowl full of jelly.

HE was chubby and plump, a right jolly old elf,

And I laughed when I saw him in spite of myself.

A wink of his eye and a twist of his head

Soon gave me to know I had nothing to dread.

He spoke not a word, but went straight to his work,

And filled all the stockings, then turned with a jerk.

AND laying his finger aside of his nose

And giving a nod, up the chimney he rose.

He sprung to his sleigh, to his team gave a whistle,

And away they all flew like the down of a thistle.

But I heard him exclaim, ere he drove out of sight—

*"Happy Christmas to all,
and to all a good night!"*

ABOUT THE POEM

Originally published as an "Account of a Visit from St. Nicholas," Moore's famous poem is often known today as "The Night Before Christmas." It first appeared on December 23, 1823, in the newspaper the *Troy Sentinel*. It was printed between an article about removing honey from a beehive and a marriage announcement. In the original version, Moore referred to two of the reindeer by their Dutch names, Dunder and Blixem. In a later version, he changed their names to Donder and Blitzen.

The poem has been reproduced throughout the world, set to music, performed as a play, made into a silent film, a CD and a video, and illustrated by award-winning artists. Except for some punctuation and spelling changes, I've followed the wording of the version first printed in the *Troy Sentinel*.

Clement Clarke Moore taught Greek and Oriental literature at the General Theological Seminary in New York City. The story goes that he wrote the poem to share with his children—eventually there were nine—on Christmas Eve. A relative copied it down and gave it to a friend in Troy, New York, who in turn sent it to the *Troy Sentinel*. The newspaper did not credit Moore as the poet, and Moore was just as glad. He was embarrassed by the poem's popularity, referring to it as "a mere trifle." Because it became so widely known, however, he finally stepped forward as the author and included it in a book of his own poems, *The New-York Book of Poetry*, published in 1837.

On October 26, 2000, an article appeared in the *New York Times* that questioned the identity of the poem's author. A professor at Vassar College, Don Foster, argued that the spirit and style of the poem were more in keeping with the verse of Henry Livingston Jr., who lived in Poughkeepsie, New York, in the 1800s.

Since no one has ever found a signed, handwritten copy of the original
poem, it's impossible to prove Foster's claim.

No matter who wrote the poem, however, it has
become an American classic. Its familiar words
warm the hearts of thousands of people
every year at Christmastime.

— *Gennady Spirin*

Written by Clement Clarke Moore
for the *Troy Sentinel*
(December 23, 1823) under the title
"Account of a Visit from St. Nicholas."

Illustrations copyright © 2006 by Gennady Spirin
All rights reserved
Marshall Cavendish Corporation,
99 White Plains Road, Tarrytown, NY 10591
www.marshallcavendish.us

LIBRARY OF CONGRESS CATALOGING-IN-PUBLICATION DATA
Moore, Clement Clarke, 1779–1863.
The night before Christmas / by Clement Clarke Moore ;
illustrated by Gennady Spirin.
p. cm.
ISBN-13: 978-0-7614-5298-0   ISBN-10: 0-7614-5298-2
1. Santa Claus–Juvenile poetry. 2. Christmas–Juvenile poetry. 3. Children's poetry, American.
I. Spirin, Gennadiæi, ill. II. Title. PS2429.M5N5 200 811'.2–dc22 2005017286

The text of this set book is set in Cochin Archaic.
The illustrations are rendered in watercolor and colored pencil.
Book design by Michael Nelson

Printed in China
First edition
2 3 4 5 6